i

c

o

p

e

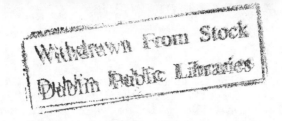

Advance Praise for Gabby Bess's
Alone with Other People

What Gabby Bess captures with her words is the beauty of a fragile time and place. In this collection, she evokes what it means to be young, to be a woman, to have both feet firmly planted both in this world and the virtual. She asks fascinating questions like, "Is anyone moved by the plainness of raw skin anymore?" She makes you trust she has the necessary answers with intelligence and confidence. In this book, Bess builds an identity for herself and tears it down and builds herself anew. It is breathtaking to behold.

**Roxane Gay, author of *An Untamed State*
and *Bad Feminist***

The poems and prose pieces in this smart and complex collection illuminate the shape of a new, 21st century webcam feminism—one that questions its own ambitions, knows the shape of pornstar mouths, and doubts the sanctity of individuality when pitted against the existential. Gabby writes with radical uncertainty about illusions of control, the limits of identity, and what it means to still want to kiss another human amidst the screenshots. This is a book that invents its own female gaze and then, like a bad bitch, breaks the lens.

Melissa Broder, author of *Meat Heart*

Gabby Bess's *Alone With Other People* orchestrates an impressive catalog of young human want with an uncompromising style. In the span between its first phrase and its last sentence, the reader is thrust forward through a virtual rolodex of self-inquisition shaped by boredom, horror, aspiration, fear for future, wonder, lust. There's a lot of intense light coming off this book full of screens and suns and large black dots.

Blake Butler, author of *Sky Saw*

Of-the-moment, brilliant, and triumphantly sad, Illuminati Girl Gang leader Gabby Bess's debut *Alone with Other People* is a post-feminist, hyper self-conscious teen swansong of the Internet age. The line between girl body and Macbook is collapsed in these vignettes that riff from blog posts, text messages, and tumblr memes, and what emerges is a "modern tragic figure who would sacrifice herself for whatever.

Kate Durbin, author of *E! Entertainment*

Don't take me for crazy when I say that the verse "Hahaha, am I alone here?" is the one that best sums up Gabby's incredible debut book, because it's true. Through each and every page that makes up *Alone With Other People*, the author manages to head out into the world with a sane, witty and protesting laugh. A laugh about the strength of woman, of youth, of poetry. When Gabby says hahaha, it also starts to unravel before our very eyes a series of texts that first and foremost find beauty in the mundane, followed by the universality of intimacy, and lastly (and most importantly): the sensation that with this book, we will never, ever feel lonely again.

Luna Miguel, author of *Bluebird and Other Tattoos*

Alone With Other People deftly deals with relationships in a highly mediated age—one that twists our perceptions of self and others. Gabby shows us how we can be simultaneously complicit in this culture but still have the desire to fight against it.

Ann Hirsch, performance artist

ALONE WITH OTHER PEOPLE

a collection of prose and poetry

GABBY BESS

For LK.

ALONE WITH OTHER PEOPLE

I WILL WRITE A NATURE POEM ABOUT FEELING GRATEFUL FOR MY MOUTH

IF INSTEAD OF ASKING ME TO INSTALL UPDATES AND RESTART MY COMPUTER I WAS ASKED IF I WANTED TO DIE INSTANTANEOUSLY I WOULD PROBABLY CLICK YES INSTEAD OF NOT NOW

GOOGLE SEARCH HISTORY: WEBMD FIBROMYALGIA, WEBMD LUMPS IN THROAT, WEBMD THROAT CANCER, HOW DO YOU KNOW IF YOU HAVE THROAT CANCER, LIKE, FOR REAL?

TRAVEL SOUTH

PUSH NOT PULL

RED GRANITE, WI

11:47 AM

EXPERIENCE THE FUN

OVERSIZED T-SHIRTS

INSIDE OF THIS POEM THERE IS A ROCK AND THEN THERE IS ME

AN EXTREMELY LONG NECK

NERVOUS CREATURES

CONGRATULATIONS, YOU OWN A LARGE ROUNDED STONE AT THE BOTTOM OF THE SEA

I am trying to improve your life by telling you these things.

I am trying to improve my life by telling you these things.

a book of mildly heartbreaking essays on continuing to wake up as yourself, despite your best efforts

ideas to get rich (#1)

15

A WOMAN WANTS WHAT A WOMAN WANTS

The alarm goes off and I wake up
to perform my critically acclaimed
sentience in my morning posture
I seek to achieve the impossible angles of a bird
laying dead in the road—with its head and its wings
folded down into the asphalt from the vantage point
of a crane shot.

To make direct eye contact
with the camera is to move the perspective from
the watched to the watcher or to present an emotion
as a publicly observable signifier,
a voyeuristic experience—
The Feel Good Movie of the Year
was my nickname in high school
and as is cinematically compelling,
I brush my teeth for the duration of sand
moving from the top of the blue plastic hourglass
to the bottom. "Look at this existence.
This pathetic, fallible, wonderful body,"
you can say rhetorically, sarcastically, or earnestly
and still achieve death.

Look at me falling in love with fallible bodies.
Look at me performing emotional labor,
my arms are strong enough
to work a tract of land:
The impatient man calls me
a bitch at my place of work
and the upward movement
of my facial muscles causes
my eyes to wrinkle, a smile.
This is a method of intention setting.

I seek a husband
with broad shoulders and a symmetrical face,
a hard worker, whose value is in the width
of his chest. I do not want
men that can teach me. There is nothing
more that I want to know; free of want,
I can't use men in the same way

16

that they can use me. "Give up
on art and love," you can say rhetorically,
sarcastically, or earnestly and still achieve death.
I wouldn't be a good wife,
but I would be a wife
in a way that was cinematically compelling.

In my dream last night
there was a factory farm
that performed full body castration;
I went there
to lay with the women who wanted
to find a calm somewhere.
I became a body
and my sentience became someone else's
problem as I awoke thinking,
"Where is my value?" as if I had misplaced
my lipstick again.

The sex can be rough
to bring pleasure with
choking & punching & the sloshing
of liquids in the back of your throat
to spit near my eye area. To reduce
my suffering, you can take my own
hands within yours
to rub the spit into my eyes &
into my mouth & you can kill me
inside of your head as many times as you need,
just to feel calm. Is anyone moved
by the plainness of raw skin anymore?

Where did this tenderness come from?

To reduce your suffering,
I will fill the inner lining of my stomach
with bullets by ingesting them like pills
until I sag heavy
& full in your hands.
The shifting of skin on skin
sounds something like an underhanded truce.
Like kissing in a trench with your fingers
crossed behind your back. I listen
as the radio plays a song about guns
Just the sound of it—the gunshot
But not an actual gunshot—a human voice
mimicking the sound of a gunshot
over a heavy beat.

*here, on your bed, is where you
spit into my mouth and onto
my face. here, on your bed,
we both became ugly. here,
in the dark spaces that allowed
me to see clearly what i was,
i wanted your ugly.*

*this image is a series of signals to your
brain that allow you to access my guilt*

PEEK-A-BOO IS A GAME THAT INFANTS ENJOY BECAUSE THEY HAVE NOT DEVELOPED OBJECT PERMANENCE

Waking alone in a room that doesn't belong to me
under a comforter that covers my entire body,
even my head, I turn into myself. The heavy folds
of sheets are disorienting.

I can feel my bangs brushing against my face
like an open palm,
covering my eyes like that game
that babies like to play to make the world disappear
and then reappear
and then fill with laughter.
Where is the second body?
Hahaha am I alone here?

At the end of her shift, Juliana walked into the bathroom to check her bangs in the mirror. Her hands were damp and marked red from various casualties throughout the day: the spill of an entire flat of fruit cups on aisle 17, the errant paper cuts from unpacking cardboard boxes, the sticky soap from a cracked bottle. In her exhaustion, she absentmindedly touched her bangs with her hands in a spastic sweeping motion across her brow, which now felt a little sticky. She imagined visible remnants from her day clinging to her hair. Juliana felt self-conscious. She felt self-conscious about her bangs. She felt self-conscious about her knees. She felt self-conscious about the fact that her name was Juliana. In 20 years she still hadn't grown into it. Her name was a foreign language that she couldn't quite say with the right accent.

Juliana stood in front of the mirror and looked at her face. Her bangs were greasier than she would have liked but she thought that they looked OK. They sat just above her eyebrows like a pair of flood pants. She felt her oversized and shapeless work-uniform crippled her, in terms of her looks, and reduced her potential for attractiveness to a mere childlike cuteness. She looked down at her nametag that read, "JULIE" in bold red letters, as she was sure to emphasize to her supervisor that she went by Julie and not Juliana. For the first week of work she wore a nametag that said "Quanique" while she waited for a nametag of her own to arrive. Juliana was Quanique for a week. Being Quanique was very similar to being Juliana except that as Quanique, Juliana felt like she could be more absurd and sarcastic inside of her head. While doing tasks at work she would think, "Quanique for a week. Quanique FOREVER" while grinning.

Although now, looking in the employee bathroom mirror, she was simply Juliana. She was Juliana Forever. She was Juliana for the entire rest of her life. The new girl that was recently hired was now Quanique on register 9. Oh, the lightness of being Quanique! When Juliana was Quanique, she was new; everything was absurd and sarcastic. Now that Juliana was just Juliana she had to come to terms with the reality of working for minimum wage. And the reality of working for minimum wage was that it was better than working for no wage but worse than other things.

Juliana wanted to pee. She didn't *have* to pee but she wanted to. (Don't be vain. Don't be so concerned with your looks, she thought.)

She reasoned that it would be good if she at least tried, if she at least sat down. In vanity there is a certain confidence and self-assurance that is unattractive in a young girl and is met with every attempt to be suppressed immediately. Even when she was alone, Juliana behaved as if she was performing for an unknown, ever-present viewer who knew what she really went in the bathroom to do. (Look at her hair. Touch her face. Consider her attributes and watch a grin form across the face reflected back to her.) She inspected her grin in the mirror: crooked, but straight from a distance. She often received compliments on her teeth. People, strangers, would say, "Oh your teeth are so straight. Did you have braces?" Juliana would reply, "Yes, but I accidentally threw away my retainer on my 10th birthday so now they are crooked" and she would try to smile real wide to show the strangers her teeth. This made her mouth appear misplaced on her face, like it was her elbow or an ill-fitting cowboy hat.

Sometimes she would look in the mirror and think, "Can I sell myself? Would anyone buy me? Am I something worth having just to look at; like a coffee table book? Just to stand inside of a living room or on top of a fireplace like an arbitrary art thing from IKEA to point at and say, 'Look at our good taste in arbitrary art things.'"

Juliana's favorite stall, if she was forced to choose something like a favorite stall, was located in the corner behind the main door to the bathroom. The door always appeared closed which made it difficult to discern if someone was already inside or not and most people moved on to the next stall without bothering to check, leaving the thick roll of toilet paper untouched and minimal amounts of pee on the floor and toilet seat. It was a safe haven for those that wanted a place to sit. Juliana closed the stall door, pulled down her pants and put her ass to the toilet seat. Her ass settled onto the toilet seat, making a suctioning sound. Juliana sat on the toilet and watched the thin rivers of piss flow through the grout lines in the tiles. Juliana counted to 10 and then flushed the toilet. Juliana un-suctioned herself from the seat and pulled up her pants.

When Juliana arrived home from work she took her MacBook into the bathroom, started the shower water and then started to undress. To Juliana, the bathroom was hers. She could sit on the toilet, doing nothing really, for hours and no one would bother her. In a family household the distinction between public and private space isn't always so clear. What was hers wasn't really hers exclusively. But the bathroom seemed to be a safe territory, a neutral zone that would protect anyone that sought asylum there.

Juliana took off her coat, her shirt and her bra. She was able to slide her pants over her thighs and back up again without unbuttoning them or unzipping them. "This is good," she thought. Juliana opened up Photo Booth and started to take pictures of her shirtless body in front of the medicine cabinet mirror. She saw the tightness of her skin over her ribs. She saw scars across her stomach with unknown origins. Juliana saw her breasts. "Not big enough for... something," she thought. She deleted all of the pictures immediately after viewing them. She viewed her life as a TV show that no one watched, or that people watched but they were bored and she knew that the show certainly wouldn't make it past the first season. Juliana imagined her funeral: a formless crowd of people in a trivial location, chatting amongst themselves, saying things like, "Oh thank God. Finally."

She stepped away from the mirror and thought, "Oh thank God. Finally."

Juliana sat down on the toilet and started to idly look at blogs and websites. She noted the shallow dent underneath the Apple logo on her MacBook, fingering the depression like an open wound and laughing while her face contorted into an ugly, sad smile like it does when she remembers ugly, sad things. Juliana thought about the day that she dented her MacBook and her face became increasingly ugly as she smiled wider and crazier while sitting on the toilet. She had trouble thinking about the past. In the past she always seemed happier. She didn't understand how time could work like that. She didn't understand how time could twist her face into an ugly, wild thing.

The dent in Juliana's MacBook appeared on the day when Adam and Juliana were laying down next to each other on Juliana's bunk bed. Adam was on the inside, closest to the wall, and Juliana was on the outside. That night Juliana was on her period and Adam kept trying to finger her while they were watching "I Love You, Man" on Juliana's MacBook. With her mouth full of Trix cereal Juliana said, "No. Not tonight," while smiling. Adam leaned in to kiss Juliana. When the movie finished, Adam and Juliana sat in silence until Adam said, "Okay, I should go." Juliana said, "No" and reached for the box of Trix. Juliana poured what was left of the Trix cereal on top of Adam's head. Juliana and Adam spent the next thirty minutes eating Trix cereal off of Juliana's sheets while laughing. After thirty minutes had passed Juliana said, "Okay, you can leave but since you're on the in-

23

side let's just barrel-roll over each other. Kind of like spies." David grinned and said, "Okay. On the count of three. You're obviously going over."

One (1)

Two (2)

Three (3)

Juliana went over, Adam went under, and Juliana's MacBook fell approximately seven feet to the ground. It hit the ground like a dead thing and bounced. Juliana felt like she didn't care about her MacBook and she laughed. She kissed Adam and wanted to have sex with him but Juliana was on her period and her roommate was on the bottom bunk the entire time.

Later on that night Adam called Juliana and said, "Come over, I have a surprise for you." Juliana biked over to Adam's apartment and found David standing in the doorway with a travel sized bottle lube much like an outdoor cat with a dead squirrel in its mouth, proud and tentative as it presented its gift. The laugh track plays.

"Since you're on your period do you want to have anal sex?" Adam grinned and Juliana stared at her feet trying to compose her face into an appropriate reaction. Juliana considered her feet. "Sure. Whatever. Whatever you want," Juliana said as she picked up her face to smile in a way that looked adventurous. Girls always have to look adventurous when propositioned with things like this.

Juliana used her MacBook approximately 16 hours a day so she thought about that story a lot. She memorized it. Edited. Highlighted details. Treating the story, along with every other sensory experience, like a third grade science experiment; naïve, at first, followed by a hopeful diligence for the desired reaction. Which object floats and which sinks in water? What separates from the oil? Juliana tried to make sense of the past year. Trying to bring it closer to the truth, or possibly further, so that when she sat in the overstuffed chair in her therapist's office and these words fell out of her mouth, her therapist would laugh instead of something worse. So that her therapist could see the lightheartedness and comfortable sweetness that possibly outweighed the manipulation and Juliana's desire to be wanted. Her therapist didn't see this. She prescribed Juliana

Klonopin, Lexapro, and Lamotrigine. Juliana put the story back in the water.

On the toilet, Juliana opened up Omegle in a tab in Safari. "You are now chatting with a stranger. Say hello. You both like [sex]." On some level Juliana didn't even like sex. On some level—one of the infinite levels that her consciousness seemed to obscure or elucidate, rather vindictively, she thought, 'at random,' causing her face to twist in discomfort at the memory of her skin being touched by another person, while she enjoyed feeling a great sadness for herself when her consciousness did choose to partially reveal how she felt about her skin being touched by another person—the act was simply a 10-45 minute relief where she didn't have to talk so much, especially if she was being choked.

She constructed herself as the modern tragic figure who would sacrifice herself for whatever.

Only once had she allowed a guy to go down on her. (Go down on her. Perform oral sex. She didn't know which term to use; one seemed to be too crude while the other seemed to be giving too much credit.) He attempted to go down on her for almost an hour and when that didn't prove profitable he drove Juliana home in silence. As they were driving, Juliana's body curled, wet, and uncomfortable, he looked down at her and said, in a matter of fact tone:

"Julie, after I drop you off I'm going to go to the hospital. I'm having an asthma attack."

Juliana instinctively thought "*good*" and then made up some joke about getting him a snorkel for next time while secretly hoping that there wouldn't be a next time but even more secretly hoping there would always be a next time. She felt her brain caving in at this thought. She felt hopeless. Juliana spent her nights like this.

Constantly caving in.

give me the means to
kill myself and i will
sever the parts of myself
that impede my progress,
including you.

gun control

THE WOMAN AT THE END OF THE CUL-DE-SAC

I watch the woman at the end of the cul-de-sac,
through my car window with the pleasure
of my internal monologue thinking "cul-de-sac"
and feeling distinctly suburban, as I drive
at slow speeds and gentle angles,
so as to not run over the deaf children that live inside
of the cul-de-sac.

The deaf children play secretly, exclusively,
a game of hide and seek, as I have never seen them
But I drive in gentle angles to feel amused and calm
thinking about humans that can go unseen

The woman at the end of the cul-de-sac
doesn't walk like a secret but she walks soft-bodied,
          like the women in poems are,
and she retrieves her mail with a small key
from the community mailbox; though she is soft-bodied
she walks without the hand of a man around her waist

The sun comes into my face
through my windshield and
I feel my internal monologue
thinking, "The Female Gaze."
I watch the words pass
inside of my head
and project
onto the sun through my eyes.
At this moment I know
that the woman in the cul-de-sac can see
the words, "The Female Gaze"
written on the sun.
Now her internal monologue is thinking,
THE FEMALE GAZE
in all caps and she feels suspicious but she pulls her face
at me to nod and smile

And I pull my face at her to nod and smile,
quickly averting my eyes before she looks to me
to improve her life or teach her something about it.
(Sometimes, my eyes suggest things about me–when

they go off talking on their own—that just aren't true,
for example,
when I was there with you on the night
that you asked me if I was sad
because my eyes were heavy and wet with tears
and I couldn't quite look at you straight on,
I was only sad
in the way that I was supposed to be
when I was there with you.)
And I know that she also averts her eyes
because the sun presents itself
as an empty light source—

We do not earn salary
for this emotional labor.

i would sleep my way to the top but the top, of whatever this is, seems like the bottom of everything else

raw ambition

Watching a documentary about Jean-Michel Basquiat,
I am revealed as an unrelenting ambition. I view
myself as an exception in a room full of people
who view themselves as an exception. To hear
someone talk of greatness and then become greatness
is the basis of American culture. I love it. It is okay
to die here. Reduction and declarative sentences
are the basis of communication. I learn it.
I teach myself
how to pronounce his name, training
myself not to say *John-Michael*
Repeating:
Michelle Michelle Michelle,
Like my mother.
Now once more, with exaggerated slowness:
JAAhn Meechelle Bask-eee-aht,
What a name for The Black Man,
like my father.

The French language becomes very ugly
when it hangs limp inside of my mouth.
To express myself in French
and sound cultured and pleasing,
is there any better way?

To master self-expression, I leave
my middle class home in Brooklyn
at 17 and become famous for cleverly expressing myself
on the sides of buildings. On the insides of art galleries
and on the cover of Artforum Magazine I express myself
fluently, with a consistent point-of-view.
I express myself to Andy Warhol
because he is my friend and he oh so
adores me!

In a documentary
about how well I was able to express myself
in my lifetime before I became addicted to
heroin and my skin became bad
and I alienated all of my friends that I had
once expressed myself to, I express myself.

30

In exchange
for expressing myself I will accept
money ($$$$$$) and hot arty-bitches
and drugs and fame and the certainty death.
Most young kings
are compensating for something.

Directing my eyes at the wall
of a home in suburban Virginia,
I concentrate my vision
in such a way until everything becomes out-of-focus
and soft and pleasing. Tell me,
what is the difference between a true occurrence
and a manipulated image?

I move the wall back into focus using my eyes, repeating:
Jahn-Michelle
Jahn-Michelle
Bask-eee-aht
Bask-eee-aht

I took up going to the library–rarely have I taken an interest
in someone other than myself, and here I can look around
and find others sitting quietly,
equally fascinated with themselves–
to read the fiction of only women
and I will take whatever advice they can offer me,
studying their diagrams. *What makes a sentence
feminine?* It must be
in the adjectives.

And so, I Googled it:

GOOD ADJECTIVES FOR WOMEN
(as written by a man):

Personality Traits
In general, there are a series of traits that have been his-
torically associated with women, such as "meekness," "shy-
ness," "calmness," "temperance," "matronly" or "compli-
ant." These terms may have a negative connotation today,
because they stem from a patriarchal society's standard for
women. Now that women are regarded as equals in society,
they are described with a broader array of adjectives, such as
"bravery," "strength," "compassion," "motivation," "humil-
ity," "meritorious," "harmonious," "artistic" or "devoted."

Unique Attributes
Positive adjectives that highlight a person's unique-
ness include these: "individual," "one-of-a-kind," "re-
markable," "noteworthy," "unmatched," "exceptional"
and "unforgettable." Keep in mind that you can use
more specific adjectives in pairs with these to describe
what makes a woman specifically unique. For example,
you could say she has remarkable and alluring eyes.

From here I constructed my identity
and set it aside for myself and others to admire.
When I give advice it is essentially saying, "Oh,
be more like me" and I can say that and point
to a diagram that I have drawn up in the time
that I have spent alone, bettering myself.

I could just go on all day pointing at things
and saying, "Just be famous"
because that is what I've worked out the goal
of life to be, I am confident in it. If I were a rich
pervert I would throw dollar bills at strangers
to make them feel famous and fulfilled.
Just be famous! Its so easy, life is so easy
when you know what you want. I'm working
toward my goal: I took all of my money
out of the bank just to roll around on it
and luxuriate in the filth of all the hands
that could touch me at once.

WHAT I CAN OBSERVE WHEN VISITING A CITY NEAR WHERE I ATTENDED HIGH SCHOOL

Walking through the Ghent district of Norfolk, VA
city blocks don't feel like
a fixed measurement. A recently erected
above-ground metro rail cuts through a road
that seems too narrow
to be a two way street
with an above-ground metro rail cutting through it.
Most days are like this:
I close my eyes to the ability
to inhabit four places
in long enough intervals
to miss them all.

The local hip-hop radio station, 103 Jamz,
is playing over the speakers in a sushi restaurant.
From the perspective of a sushi restaurant window,
there is a homeless man walking confidently
across the street in one direction
while smiling. He turns around and walks back
across the street in the other direction. He is still
smiling. On the drive home I get lost trying
to find a highway that goes North.
At one point, I end up on a farm
where the edges of the property open
up to meet the Potomac river & at another
point I end up at a police training facility.
I arrive at both places and think,
"Let me stay here." There is too much
smiling in the back of the van that is driving
parallel to me. There are too many faces
that look exactly the same
when pressed against a tinted window
moving at the speed of 70 miles per hour
on a highway at night.

Paige spilled milk onto her kitchen floor on purpose. She thinks, "I am doing this. The milk. My hands and my brain are allowing me to do this. This must be okay, if I can physically do this. My body was made for this," as the milk goes from inside of the carton to the floor. Paige thought of everything that her body was physically able to do. Paige could murder. Paige could scream at an uncomfortably loud volume to others around her and even herself. Paige could masturbate until her body became whatever bodies become when they get too tired and sad and they give up completely. At any point in her life, Paige thought, she could say fuck it and completely give herself over to the physicality of her body. She could become all movement and motion and impulse. On this day, when this day happens, Paige thought, she would improve her posture. She would let her shoulders roll back and her neck extend. She would allow her body to appear confident and tall. Paige wanted to perform the physical limitations of her body like a community theatre play, aware of her own thinly concealed artifice. Paige lifted her shoulders up to her ears and then slammed them down. She did this exactly five times. She wanted to make sure that her shoulders were locked into place. Paige lifted her right arm incrementally until it was outstretched in front of her face. She spread each of her fingers apart until her palm felt vulnerable. She stood in the middle of the kitchen with her arm outstretched as she watched the white milk blend into the white tiled floor. Paige watched the milk seemingly disappear against the floor, find a pathway through the tile grout and zigzag its way underneath the refrigerator. Paige's feet stayed dry and everything remained normal. "Inconsequential," thought Paige, "like most things." Paige let her body collapse in on itself as she slumped down into a hard wooden chair.

Paige sat down at the kitchen table and stared at her iPhone. She touched the screen and tried to will messages to appear. She was waiting for something, anything, to happen. Lately Paige felt as though she simply allowed things to happen to her rather than proactively trying to set in motion a series of events. She had taken to letting events and other people set her in motion, in any motion, in any direction. Not only was she willing to go wherever something happened to take her, she simply no longer cared. Paige told this to her therapist. Her therapist replied by shrugging her shoulders noncommittally and saying, "This too shall pass."

Paige was waiting for a text, or any acknowledgement of her existence, from Adam. Paige and Adam had been dating for five months. The last time Paige saw Adam was exactly a week ago.

Adam and Paige sat together in the front seat of Paige's car parked in the driveway of their apartment. Paige sat in the driver's seat with her back against the car door and her legs draped across Adam's lap. In the passenger's seat, Adam held a small plastic bag with JWH, a synthetic cannabinoid, inside of it. He rested the plastic bag on Paige's legs as he reached forward to grab the pack of Lucky Strikes that sat patiently on the dashboard, its red and white cardboard exterior wilting in the constant July heat. Adam took two cigarettes out of the box, licked the ends of them with his tongue, and dipped them into the bag of powder. This method of smoking JWH is known as "tipping." Paige's first experience with tipping was not pleasant. The first time Paige smoked JWH she was standing on the balcony of Adam's apartment. Adam and Paige shared a cigarette that was laced with JWH while they drank forties in their underwear. Paige kept hallucinating a light consistently flashing on the brick wall of the hotel building and she felt paranoid that the flashing light was a man on a bicycle that kept riding by, three stories above ground, just to watch Paige in her underwear. But now she feels calm whenever she smokes JWH. Time feels slower for her. She could live inside the pocket of every second just a little bit longer. It gave her time to breathe.

Adam handed Paige one of the cigarettes and they smoked while listening to the radio. This had become a daily ritual. Lately, however, it seemed like there was always something preventing them from just sitting closely together in comfortable silence. Adam had been acting increasingly distant and seemed to have other things that he would rather do. Paige and Adam scanned the radio stations for contest announcements or free giveaways. Today, in the next town over, a car dealership was having a test drive promotion. If you were one of the first 100 people, the radio announced, to get to the dealership and test drive a car you could win a $35 gift card. Adam idly played with the skin on Paige's knees. "Should we do that? Do you think it's too late to be in the top 100?" he asked while grinning. Paige laughed. "I don't know. I can't tell the time. It feels like they announced that hours ago. We should just sit here. Your hands are on my legs and I just want them to stay there." Adam's hands felt heavy on Paige's legs and she felt as if she had molded to the seat of the car. In that moment she didn't mind the idea of being a permanent part of her car. She wanted to sit like that for a long time.

"We could do a lot with $35 though," said Adam. "We could basically be millionaires at the dollar store." "We could be thirty-five-dollara-naires," Paige said. Paige looked down at her legs. They felt lighter. Adam's hands were now adjusting the dials on the radio. Adam became silent and shifted his body away from Paige.

Alone in her kitchen, Paige's iPhone began to vibrate. Paige looked down at her iPhone but it was not Adam that was causing this disturbance. Paige had received a text from her ex-boyfriend, Adam 2, wishing her a happy birthday. Paige had a conversation with Adam 2 via text message. She learned that his most recent girlfriend had broken up with him for seemingly "no reason."

"I feel like my life is on a shitty loop," Adam 2 said via text message. "Every time I feel as if I have transcended the loop and start to think 'this time it's going to be different, life takes a dump on the still idealistic parts of me. Maybe I am depressed. Well, I am definitely depressed. But I am in mourning."

"I feel like life is mainly a shitty loop," Paige responded. "I feel unsure of this though. I am on three different mood stabilizers so I don't think I experience a full range of emotions anymore. I feel abstractly dissatisfied with my life but mostly detached."

Paige wondered if this was what it was supposed to feel like, if this was just life, if this was statistical normalcy. She wondered if blankness was merely contentedness. Maybe, without knowing, Paige had accidentally settled into happiness. She wasn't sure of this. Even without feeling sad, Paige knew that she was sad. Paige was convinced that she was lacking something that everyone else had, something that she did not even have the innate capacity to fathom. Paige wanted to run down to the street and ask everyone she encountered what this thing was or what it could possibly be. What is inside of you besides this human stuff of veins and bones and existential longing?

"Why does everything eventually become terrible?"

Paige thought about this. It was seemingly a non sequitur but she assumed that Adam 2 was referring to his recent breakup. Why do relationships become terrible? Before Paige could respond, Adam 2 texted, "People give up too easily." Do relationships start to disintegrate when the people in them simply stop trying to hold them together? *If a relationship needs to be so carefully held and attend-ed to, is it fated to fail from the start?* Paige tried to formulate a con-ception of love and relationships. She wasn't sure if "not giving up" was the main strategy for keeping a relationship's vital signs healthy. Paige thought that, almost by design, it is hard not to feel alienated from another person no matter what and that, she thought, is what makes relationships so difficult. A human brain is encased in a skull and each human exists in separate body so it seems like there is al-ways going to be a feeling of disconnect; one human will never com-pletely understand what another human is thinking or feeling. Paige felt increasingly lonely as she thought about how she would never be able to make anyone understand what she was thinking or feeling.

Paige knew that Adam 2 was a romantic. He believed in an all-en-compassing love. He believed that love was a force, similar to a God, which was bigger than humanity, bigger than loneliness, bigger than alienation. She knew that in every relationship, including theirs, Adam 2 believed that not only had his partner failed him, but they had failed love.

Paige believed that love was not just an unquantifiable thing. Paige thought of love as twofold. She thought that love was made up of an immeasurable amount of concrete things about one's partner and about oneself and about the interaction between the two. She thought of love as the overarching combination of all of those things that make you feel emotionally endeared to the other person. Then, she thought, under the overarching endearment is the day-to-day minutia; the concrete and tangible. It is possible that although one may feel this overarching love for their partner they may not neces-sarily feel, on a concrete level, that they are compatible. They may feel completely emotionally attached from their partner but not fully content simply discussing the boring minutia of their lives. Paige thought that in this way it seemed understandable for someone to 'give up' on love when at the point in the relationship the overarch-ing feeling of love becomes vague and distant. All that is left is just minutia and coexistence that, unfortunately, are not aligned.

Paige's iPhone vibrated and then lit up in her hands. The screen dis-played a text message from Adam that said, "I haven't been feeling well lately." "I've been trying to figure out what's going on with you," Paige responded, "and you don't talk to me about how you feel or anything that's going on with you. When I'm not feeling well I want to talk to you about it because you make me feel better. But apparently when you're not feeling well you want nothing to do with me. What am I doing that makes you feel that way?" Adam said that he just felt shitty and wasn't really interacting with anyone lately. When you're stressed, Paige thought, you want to go to comforting things. You want to be around and talk only to the people that make you feel good and comfortable. By this logic, Paige could only assume that this distance was because she was no longer a person that made Adam feel good and comfortable.

Paige attempted to question Adam as to why he was being despondent and evasive. She approached the situation from sadness—from complete bewilderment and ignorance as to why he would act this way. Paige had a sadness that was so desperate that it could not yet turn into anger. This sadness did not yet know how to be angry. Paige knew that a reaction of anger chanced the possibility that she would only receive anger in return. She knew that her anger could turn her into "the crazy girlfriend." Paige did not have the privilege of anger, no matter how deserved. Anger could cause her legitimate, rational, and rightful questions to be ignored. Paige's chest started to tighten and she could feel the anxiety physically overwhelming her body. Slowly, as if her own mind wanted to torture her with what was about to happen. Paige closed her eyes and thought about the white milk against the white floor. Inconsequential, she tried to remind herself. She knew that this was happening, this crushing feeling inside her ribcage and between her lungs, but she also knew that it would stop happening and that other things would happen, eventually.

[image of us playing solitare on a wooden floor]

at night we could look so happy

THE THEMATIC CONTENT OF 1AM TEXTS

My roommate
is out of town.

Let's do something
that will make us feel
less alone.

Adam and I are in a hospital.

Adam is conscious and only slightly injured.

I am slightly there in the memory of Adam's hospital room, looking in from the wooden kitchen table of his childhood home that fits the expanse of our two bodies, peripherally touching, like a bed that we share
for the first time.

We visit Adam's parents' house and this prompts him to tell me more of his clumsy childhood.

I keep Adam's stories and I keep my own, still afraid to trust someone with my vulnerability.

Adam, 23, lays his head on my lap and Adam's face, age 8, is able to grimace and his nerves can still send pain signals to his brain.

The doctor prods at his arm with a metal object:

"Does this hurt?"

"Yes."

"Does *this* hurt?"

"Yes."

He is only eight years old.

He only recently learned how inline roller-skate and 30 minutes ago he learned that golden retrievers could seem like bears when they are chasing him on the road behind his house.

In the bed next to his, separated by a curtain partition, there is a woman dancing in a coma.

Well, not dancing but just kind of laying still with her eyes closed, being very quiet, and taking fluids intravenously; she is drooling, but less than one would think. If one ever thinks about a coma patient's drool output.

But Adam doesn't think of that because he is eight years old and he is scared, but excited.

He thinks about how he is going to be able to wear a brightly colored cast.

He thinks about being very popular when he goes back to school the next week.

In a memory I watch him as an eight year old and I watch him now, at 23, laying next to me as I pet his head. Our bodies are oriented as crushed bones on the opposite of whatever.

His healed arm wraps around my body to pull me closer.

On the drive to Adam's apartment we discuss the proper protocol for drug deals after posing the philosophical question:

What should you do if your drug dealer doesn't text you back?

Should I text him again? Does the three-day rule apply in this situation?

We drive past the gas station and u-turn on a one-way street.
In front of the 7-11 we stand dumbly when the doors do not open automatically for us. Amazed that there is something outside of us that will not let us in.

Outside of his apartment the neighborhood cat sleeps under a car.

I bend down to look at the sleeping cat. I watch her suffer from the constraints of being a soft, fuzzy, hand-sized thing.

I know that she does not want to be touched.

I used to grab at her and she would run to pick at dead things at the far end of the parking lot.

She is happier there, with the dead things, than she would be underneath my needy palm.

At 7-11 we bought toothbrushes and orange juice and now, in the dark of Adam's room, I watch him brush his teeth.

"Did you smoke today?" I ask.

"Yes. But it's your fault. You weren't around to distract me with better vices."

We made a deal that day:
Every time he wanted to smoke a cigarette, we would have sex instead.

I am tired.

That night, when I am naked and he is clothed, his eyes become scared and hungry.

He turns to me and says, "You make me believe in God and holidays, if God and holidays are abstractions for intense longing."

Tenderly rubbing over my thighs and my back, he tells me that he just doesn't know what to do with me, like I am a problem to be endured or dealt with.

I turn to lay on my back, eyes flirting furiously with the ceiling tiles. I am quiet.

Still curved towards me, he tells me about how he would like to have a child with me so that it could be beautiful.

"*Love, love, love,*" he hums. He is singing the words to a song that I do not know.

He remembers the episode of The Conan O'Brien Show where Conan O'Brien becomes an ordained minister for free online so that night the two of us become ordained ministers for free through an online Universalist Unitarian church.

With our newfound powers, we marry the tables to the chairs and the bedside lamp to the nightstand using The Naked Lunch as a bible stand-in.

Tonight everything has joined in union, arbitrarily. The bedside lamp did not protest to its new life on the nightstand. I feel happy but not in love. But I don't feel sad so, as a wife, I sleep well.

THINGS THAT I PUT INTO SARAH'S MOUTH

I.

"The only girl I ever loved was born with roses in her eyes..." The song with that lyric plays on the outdoor speakers, sounding something like summertime, like cherries under my thumbnails and red dripping down the front of my blouse. But in the mountains it is cold. There are tea lights that are dim. In the woodshed behind Sarah's house there is a small purple something hanging from a chair:

"Why do you have such a small belt? Is it a baby belt?"

"No... it's a dog belt."

We laugh and forget the word for collar.

We run out of the shed, past a lake and a family graveyard. We don't know those bones but I know what it feels like to know a dead girl. Her text messages are in my phone. I don't look at them but I keep them there. It seems fucked up to delete a dead girl's texts. It seems pointless. She is already gone. I know that it is only productive to think of what is here. Only what is here can think of me. But still, I think about the dead girl while I look at the girl sitting next to me, on a bench suspended from a tree. Sarah is like the dead girl, like me. Bipolar.

"Sarah."

"Yeah?"

"Do you want to switch?"

I trade the carrot that I am smoking out of for Sarah's apple. She asks me if I want to shotgun. I nod my head up and down and the motion causes my face to feel cold. I feel excited to touch Sarah's lips. Sarah takes a hit from the carrot and inhales. I press my lips, slightly opened, against hers as she exhales into my mouth.

II.

I'm on campus a day earlier than the last day of winter break. I walk up two flights of steps to get from my second floor dorm room to

46

Sarah's third floor dorm room. I knock on the door and hope that she is on campus a day earlier than the last day of winter break too. Sarah opens the door. She is wearing plaid flannel pajama pants and a grey tank top. I ask her if she wants to walk around or sit or stand or lay down with me. We decide to walk. I watch her put on jeans and a sweater.

We walk to the 7-11 and then we walk through the Crim Dell Meadow. We sit in the leaves next to two bronzed statues of a couple in love. The guy statue is lying down on his side and the girl statue is sitting upright. She is reading a letter. Sarah and I mimic their poses and eat black pepper kettle chips.

Sarah takes out a pack of lucky strikes and talks about pelicans and the 50s. Her face becomes animated and she uses her hands to make pelicans and abstract art in the air in front of our faces. She talks about how her grandfather locked himself in his basement and drew portraits of pelicans from memory until he died. She lifts up her shirt to show me a pelican tattoo that I've seen before. I look at the tattoo again and I take the cigarette out of Sarah's mouth and place it into the mouth of the statue. We watch the statue smoke and think about taking an Instagram picture.

III.

In the attic of our building we sit on an old couch and watch a show about pets that have killed their owners but Sarah isn't really paying attention to the show about pets that have killed their owners. She is on her laptop showing her breasts and her ass to strangers on Chatroulette. I throw pieces of popcorn at Sarah's body to try to win over her attention from strangers on the Internet. Sarah turns to me and concentrates on my hand. I lob a piece of popcorn into the air and she catches it in her mouth.

"Where did you get the popcorn?"

"I found it on the floor next to the couch. It should be OK."

After a few minutes Sarah becomes bored of Chatroulette and interested in the show about pets that have killed their owners. We both eat the floor popcorn and watch the TV as a man is eaten alive by his pet komodo dragons. We then watch as the komodo dragons subsist off of his flesh until the police arrive, weeks later.

go back in time
to warn self
about self.

(if possible)

HOW TO LIVE

On the edge of my bathtub I watch a girl
lick cum off of her face and smile.

I can cry while watching porn when it reminds me of sex
with someone that I loved who now loves somewhere else.
When the girl in the video kind of does something
that she thinks is sexy but the guy laughs instead of thinking it's sexy.
When the sex is slow and it takes some time
to figure out how to change positions without pulling out.

My heart pushes up this heart stuff. I can feel it
when strangers that look like us are fucking.
We exist somewhere in there.

Everyone was happy,
even if it was only for a very brief period of time.
Repeat this 30 times.

I saw a small boy, probably six or seven,
petting his dog on the side of a suburban road.
He seemed happy.

I turned left across a four-lane road.
Two lanes headed southbound.
Two lanes headed northbound.
Or east or west my sense of direction is confused.
A smiling woman in a sad blue car sped up behind me
swerved around me, turned left before the light turned red,
then crashed into a pole.

On the courtyard of a liberal arts campus
a guy, a twenty-something, is giving a tour to prospective freshmen.
A girl, not quite a twenty-something, walks across the courtyard.
The tour guide turns from his group of prospective freshmen
and points to the girl walking across the courtyard.
She smiles like a smoker and waves with one hand
while she uses the other to hold her sundress down against the wind.
The tour guide turns back to his group of prospective freshmen
and says,

"I have found the person that I want to spend the rest of my life with."
All of a sudden it smells like vanilla.

BAD BITCH

We mapped out every conceivable route
through the subways of New York
in our search to find Jay Z to show him
our poetry, unsolicited. In the process
our bodies shrunk, feeling humbled.
After a period of 3 to 6 months,
Jay Z politely declined our poetry in a form
rejection letter that I printed out and framed
and often look at now as it sits on the edge of my desk
in my corner office with a view. I look back
on the whole thing fondly and have a laugh
with you as we catch up over drinks.

Here is a graph:
I call you a bitch in a way that means 'Girl Power'
Jay Z calls you a bad bitch in a way means 'Dope Girl'
From what we were to CEOs
Of The Word Bitch,
we started from the bottom
and now we are still at the bottom,
buried in a mattress like drug money.

That night we felt empowered to stand
on the bar singing, LADIES IS PIMPS TOO
and I GIVE UP ON LIFE. Damn, I took it
so much to heart that I couldn't even sleep with
those words inside of my chest.
Nearing 4am I was still taking pictures of my veins
through the near-translucent skin on my breasts
and the undersides of my forearms to place
in an eBay listing. I sold my blood
for its street value: The Blood of a Young-Girl
          The money
I received is harmless and secret, buried in
a mattress that I have diagrammed here:
This portion is for the dollar
This portion is for feminism
This portion is for The Blueprint 1-3
This portion is for sleeping
This portion is for turning, sleepless

WE CAN PLAY THAT GAME WHERE WE PRETEND THAT WE ARE IN A DOCUMENTARY ABOUT THE INTRICACIES OF HUMAN RELATIONSHIPS

Is "sell out" still a dirty word?
Because that's what I'm going to name my first born child, if it's a girl
or a stack of 100 dollar bills.

A tiny human that expresses
wanting emotions using crying
and nonsense syllables
is called a baby—
Tight like a baby
Small dick like a baby
Soft like a baby
Innocent like a baby
Cry like a baby
New like a baby
Accidental like a baby
Closed eyes like a baby
You call me baby
and in your hands that is what I become
as we sit cross-legged on your bed,
bare mattress to carpet,
watching TV shows on my MacBook
because you can't afford furniture yet.

Laughing inwardly at the NBC comedy Thursday lineup,
our knees express wanting emotions as they bump together.
We know that these shows won't last another season
but we are laughing now and next year
we can laugh about something else.

With both hands
I hold the large, pale orange
that we shoplifted from Whole Foods
earlier that day.

You take the large orange from me
and in your hands it becomes
a tiny grapefruit

I FEEL OF GREAT IMPORTANCE, HISTORICALLY

Something unnamable pushes against our faces
and overtakes us,
creating the womblike sensation that we knew of
before birth and that I can sometimes remember
when you hold me here, like this:
[I position my arms
around myself to show you what you look like
and what I feel like. It is inefficient and unilluminating.]
To the same effect, I try to communicate
several specific ideas in this way, with my arms
performing useless actions at you.
I feel of great importance, historically,
when you manage to look at me with some understanding,
even if it is only out of politeness. Our bodies
can only exhibit actions as outcome of movement,
this is our unfortunate way of being. Though my intention
was to move closer to you, you view me as far away
in some distant space doing curious, indiscernible,
things with my arms.
From some distant space, I am still trying
to communicate with you. This time, through a long email
that patiently delineates the plot of a movie with
characters that remind me of us, and includes helpful links
to starred reviews and the movie's IMDb page.

what do you do when you tell someone that you love them and they say, "i am reading a history of north korea entitled 'under the loving care of the fatherly leader'"?

recent google searches (#1)

Adam was always sending Caitlin quotes from books that she hasn't read and probably will never read.

They used quotes as a form of conversation because they didn't have anything else to say to each other.

Instead of talking about current events, pop culture, or emailing YouTube video links back and forth, Adam and Caitlin talked about the past. The unchanging events of fictional characters with lives that were more interesting than their own.

Adam liked to point out quotes that seemed to abstractly apply to their current situation.

Through Adam, Caitlin has read Phillip Roth:

["This made me laugh," Adam said.]

"Just as I am about to unlock the door, imagining I have covered my tracks, my heart lurches at the sight of what is hanging like snot to the toe of my shoe. I am the Roskolnikov of jerking off—the sticky evidence is everywhere!"

["It has a section titled 'Cunt Crazy'. The son has a literal Oedipal fixation on his mother. It is written in stream-of-consciousness self-loathing Jewish-American prose. What is with male writers and their cocks? I've never felt the urge to write about jacking off. But it is a perennial fixation for Updike and apparently Phillip Roth."

Caitlin said, "I think writing is not dissimilar to masturbation."]

Under the Loving Care of the Fatherly Leader: North Korea and the Kim Dynasty by Bradley K. Martin:

"North Korea called Carter a 'vicious political mountebank;' his journey, 'a powder-reeking trip of a hypocrite agitating for aggression and war.' But a North Korean spokesman in Tokyo said that, in the North Korean lexicon, this was a relatively moderate slur. At least the North had not called Carter an imperialist, its worst insult.'

["Not an imperialist! Anything but that!" For three days they joked in mock horror about the thought of being called an imperialist. Adam brought up the joke recently and Caitlin groaned in return.]

The Marriage Plot by Jeffery Eugenides:

"He held up the baggie. Leonard stuck his nose into the bag and his depression lifted another notch. It smelled like the Amazonian rain forest, like putting your head between the legs of a native girl that had never heard of Christianity."

[Adam called it a 'paltry piece of fiction' but he said that he wanted to put his head between her legs and Caitlin said "okay" even though she had no intention of letting him do that. Caitlin remembered the first time he went down on her in the hotel room that Adam lived in at the time. It was the first time Caitlin had oral sex. It was the first time someone had done something specifically for her for more than an hour. Adam kept looking up at her periodically with this apologetic look on his face. Caitlin kept looking at his bed sheets, trying to figure out the thread count with a concerned enough look on her face that could have hopefully been misconstrued as a look of pleasure.]

Once, he texted Caitlin and said, "I must fuck you."

Caitlin didn't reply but she took a screen shot of the text. She texted him the screenshot a few days later without context.

This was the only quote Caitlin had ever sent him. She sent it in a way that meant:

"Look at all the ridiculous things you say to me." He took it to mean she wanted to sext.

This was the conversation when Adam mentioned to Catlin that she would be good at writing erotica and then made sure to add that he was too much of a book snob to read erotica. Though, while Caitlin was sending him detailed descriptions of how she masturbated (face down, sometimes with lesbian porn) he didn't seem to mind erotic realism.

One night Adam texted Caitlin,

"Intense solitude becomes unbearable only when there's nothing one wishes to say to another."

He texted Caitlin again before she answered and told her that the quote is from *Americana* by Don Delillo.

Caitlin looked at her iPhone light up and then checked her Gmail.

While she was going through her spam inbox, trying to figure out how to get off all of these subscription lists (Macy's, PETA, Sierra Club, ModCloth, Urban Outfitters) that she thought were a good idea to sign up for at the time, Adam texted her a third time and said something like,

"I just finished a margarita. I am dining at alone at Plaza Azteca."

He had perfectly crafted a scenario within the span of three text messages of a lonely drunk writer, drinking comically tropical drinks in a Mexican restaurant, while contemplating the prose of the American heartland. In the back of his mind, behind his wire-framed glasses, matted, self-conscious beard, and nervously thin lips, Caitlin just knew that he thought this was a romantic vision of a struggling writer that drinks margaritas until drunk or out of cash and eats vegetarian tacos because they are cheaper.

Bukowski in paradise.

Adam quoted Bukowski too often to keep count. It was mostly in reference to how he was so much like him or how he had thought that drinking at 3 am on a Tuesday while writing self-loathing poetry made him so much like him. Caitlin usually waited until about the fifth text in a row to text him back when Adam started his Bukowski rants. She knew that the important part wasn't that she had anything to say back; the important part was to make him feel like someone else thought he was like Bukowski; his little dark girl with kind eyes. Caitlin always wanted to tell him that she hated Bukowski. Maybe he is kind of like Bukowski, Caitlin thought.

Caitlin texted back, "I like that quote." Even though she didn't really like that quote. Caitlin liked to sit alone and not talk about how she was sitting alone. She liked to drink to get drunk then go to sleep in her own bed. She didn't mind not having anything to say.

Immediately Adam responded, "I knew you would. I want you. Come to me." Caitlin did not want to drink margaritas with him. She did not want to talk in quotes. She did not want to be the kind of person that brings novels to Mexican restaurants. She did not want to be with the kind of person that thinks bringing a novel to a Mexican restaurant makes them an interesting person. Some nights, she just wanted to talk about the weather. Some nights, she really didn't care what was and what wasn't post-modern. Some nights, she wished that she and Adam were *post-conversation*. She wished that they didn't have to turn everything into a metaphor for itself.

Adam once told Caitlin that she was his 'manic pixie dream girl' like he had never even spoken to her before as if she was a caricature of herself or a trope to be employed in one of his short stories. He could never talk to her like she was in the present tense.

Caitlin knew that if she met him at Plaza Azteca she would spend the entire evening playing a game with herself. She would take sips from her glass of water and try to figure out ways to hide it from the waiter. She would want to see the cup completely empty. No water, no ice. If the waiter asked to refill her glass she would have to oblige. Those were the rules. She would perform her water dance while Adam would talk to her about something he read or wanted to read (something about Gore Vidal or Salman Rushdie) and he wouldn't notice what Caitlin was doing with her water. Caitlin would think silently about how many water-related quotes he had, quotes about being empty.

Caitlin texted him "K" and drove over to Plaza Azteca.

STEVE BUSCEMI EYES

Supine, I am watching TV.
In the dark, light moves against the wall
behind me as the scenes change on the TV
and nothing else happens
but night turning back into day. I witness it:
The nothingness, the feeling of wasting my day
off from work. I think about ingesting caffeine
to make myself more of a person
that is motivated and interested in life.
5 am on a Friday is a time that doesn't exist to me
when I can sleep and my father is pulling
the trash can out onto the sidewalk.
Tonight/This Morning I have a distinct sense
of 5am and sadness in my stomach as I lay supine
but I can't cry like this
because of gravity, maybe. Who do I need
to email to improve my life?
When Kanye says, "Ain't no tuition for having
no ambition/and there ain't no loans
for sittin your ass at home," he is making
eye contact with me.

Outside there is a singular bird
seemingly shrieking out
into nothing, performing the sadness
that I project onto her. It sounds
like a nervous breakdown,
I know this. I feel it
in the vibrato and the tree
branches, given temporary meaning,
clutched by light bird feet,
feel an immense sense of duty
to console. Feeling an immense
sense of duty, I want to call back to her
but the bird wouldn't understand
that she wasn't alone. There is nothing
I can immediately do
to fulfill my sense of duty to everything
that is suffering. Keep in mind,
that I would hurt someone
if I knew who to hurt. Am I

the ultimate goodness?

On the TV,
Steve Buscemi looks sad, the way his eye folds sag,
though he smiles and laughs
with slicked back hair.
He waits tables through the TV screen,
making the lights move on the wall behind me.
I lay and I watch him
I feel myself not cry
I hear the bird shriek
and then become apologetic sounding:
softer, slower, desperate,
and then silent to my ears.

But the bird can shriek at differing decibels,
heard or unheard to me, and I can only remain
supine; Steve Buscemi can always wait tables
through the TV screen like this,
even in death,
and I can watch him.

capitalize on generalized, widespread, anxiety

ideas to get rich (#1A)

On your bed
we sit like miniature bears.

You can bury me in your mattress, I want to
sit next to you until we become dangerous.
Until we become parade balloons of bears,
cut loose and floating too close
to the street level floors of buildings.

"I want you up there,"
you said with closed eyes, pointing
to the light fixture that you called a ceiling necklace
when you couldn't think of the word chandelier.

Well, cross your heart and hope to live
for a very long time.

Painted onto the wall tiles, the whales are on clouds
and their bodies are clouds too.
Sometimes I press my head against the shower wall
and cry quietly into them.

I'm alone here, with the whales.
I can think of anything and still be alone.
I wrote this poem and now I am alone with
this poem, the whales, and the abstractly formed thoughts
that I've already forgotten about. These words
that I write don't compare to what I've imagined
you to feel like. Pressing into it,
I am a powerful force amongst whales.

I feel like my anti-depressants are working.

THE UNIVERSE HAS TAUGHT US A GREAT TRICK

Lately all of Jane's friends had been swallowing themselves whole. This was the conclusion that Jane came to when all of her friends seemingly disappeared from her life. This was particularly inconvenient for Jane because at midnight it would be Jane's 20th birthday. It was 10 pm on the east coast and in her apartment on the east coast, Jane lay on the wooden floor with her iPhone suspended above her face, held by her hands. Jane stared at her iPhone wondering who she could text. "They have all eaten themselves," Jane declared sadly as she scrolled through the contacts in her phone alphabetically. Adam, IT Administration, Olivia Aiken, air1magic, Alice, Amtrak, gone, gone, gone, gone, gone. Jane felt alone.

Jane tried to convince herself that her friends would not leave her on purpose. Maybe, all of Jane's friends had orchestrated this great prank against her to surprise her on her birthday. They had orchestrated this prank just to show Jane what great friends they were and since they were great and fabulous friends they could joke around on such a high level. Maybe, Jane thought, her friends would materialize themselves inside of her apartment at exactly midnight, with their faces flushed red, teeming with excitement, at finally seeing Jane after having to hide from her for so long. They would run up to her, all arms and embraces, as they told her all about the illusion that they had learned. "Look, Jane" they would say, "The universe taught us a great trick. We can swallow ourselves whole and return again. We have returned just for you. Nothingness was wonderful but we are deeply sorry that we left you to exist alone."

The trees and the darkness outside of Jane's window obscured her view of the street below. The trees stood like a scared improv troupe performing something called, "The World Still Exists Outside of Your Window." For all she knew, her whole street could have swallowed itself to feed the universe's intense hunger. Jane didn't know how to comprehend the universe. She imagined the universe as a giant sad thing that consistently felt alienated by itself because it was too large and too sad for anyone to possibly understand it. Jane felt bad for the universe. Maybe the universe needed her friends more than she did. But then Jane thought about how it didn't make sense to feel bad for the universe—the universe was just chemicals, she decided—and with that she felt bad for herself again.

When something swallows itself there are no remains. Whatever was, simply returns to nothingness. Jane sat in her small apartment surrounded by nothingness. Everything inside of her apartment remained normal. Jane shifted her eyes without moving her head to look at the expanse of her apartment. Her couch was sitting in the middle of the naked wood floor. The lamps, end tables, and various stacks of evidence of Jane's existence remained completely still. Jane positioned herself on her back on the wooden floor. Lying on the floor, she lifted her leg up as far as it could go. Jane was not very flexible so her leg did not go very far. She bent her leg at the knee and curled her abdomen to try to coerce her foot closer to her mouth. Jane stretched her mouth wide and wildly thrusted her leg toward her head and her head toward her leg. This caused Jane to roll around on the floor like a dumb happy dog. Jane could not swallow herself whole. Jane laid out like a starfish in defeat. "I'm an asshole starfish," Jane thought. While rolling across the floor, Monday had turned into Tuesday and Jane had turned 20. Jane's friends had noticeably not materialized in her apartment. Since Jane could not swallow herself she attempted to do the opposite. Jane lay across the floor of her apartment and tried to make her body 1 million feet long, pushing her body into every corner and crevice, to fill up the empty space. "I am the biggest asshole starfish," Jane thought.

*love is hiding out
with my car keys*

always too late

SELL ME SOMETHING

There's a joke somewhere
in the fact that when someone calls my house phone
and the caller ID is unknown/blocked
the automated voice on the phone says
"Call from... Unavailable"

Haha call *for* Unavailable, more like it
I just let the phone ring or move farther
away from it

I don't know.
I'm not skilled
at expressing my sadness with humor
so I will express my sadness
with sadness.
I guess
there's a joke somewhere
in the fact that I still have a house phone
and the only people that call it are confused
or trying to sell me something

On Monday, Jeanne woke up for work. Just as she had the day before and just as she would in the days to follow. On Monday, as on any other day of the week, Jeanne worked at Target. The thing about working at a large retail franchise is that it sucks. There were small moments when Jeanne paused and she could feel herself becoming a machine; only slightly more personable and fallible than a computer. She could feel herself instinctively knowing exactly what aisle, shelf, and position a specific product was placed when asked. Another thing about working in a large retail franchise is that you wake up each morning and think, "OK. This is my life," with a little less shock and distress as the days move forward and your life remains stagnant.

There aren't many career choices for a depressed college dropout but as a woman, Jeanne felt that she had been training for work in retail her entire life. Jeanne learned to perform emotional labor, to smile when approached, to ask what could be done to help, to provide that help and care. Jeanne learned to have an automated response available when asked, "How are you?" The answer is, "I'm fine. Thank you." However, as a woman, as an employee, you are the first to ask, "How are you?" Always ask first. Always respond when called sweetie or honey. Sweetie. Honey. Baby girl. As a woman, those were also her names. Jeanne never had any experience in retail but she had known what to do and what to expect her whole life.

Before work, Jeanne made pasta for breakfast. In the kitchen it was quiet and the linoleum floor felt cold underneath her bare feet. The click of the gas stove attempted to signal the kitchen to life as Jeanne turned on the stove to boil water. The sun struggled to enter the windows but Jeanne had shut the blinds tight. There was a sad glow against walls caused by the kitchen light fixture that was turned on the dimmest setting. A feeling of being watched settled over Jeanne and hung over her. Suddenly she felt like she was the subject of a film and she became careful. Jeanne could imagine how the film of her life would begin:

> There is an overhead shot of the boiling pasta with her hand stirring it. The lighting, her hand, and the things on her hand slightly change seven times to indicate that everyday she boils water for pasta and it is just as quiet.

At work Jeanne focused intently on folding towels into geometrically perfect rectangles. While she was folding towels a Jamaican woman with a thick accent approached Jeanne and asked her where "the dutch" was. Jeanne felt confused as to what she was referring to. "You know," the Jamaican woman said, "the dutch... for your coochie" and the Jamaican woman pointed to her crotch.

When it was time for her scheduled 15-minute break Jeanne walked past the shampoo isle on her way toward the breakroom. She noticed a coworker that she had not yet spoken to. Jeanne had noticed him before. From his nametag she had discerned that his name was Kenneth. Kenneth sat on the floor of the shampoo isle for eight hours and stacked bottles of shampoo all day, as his only job was to arrange the shampoos. Kenneth had Down's syndrome.

Jeanne only vaguely knew how Down's syndrome actually affected a person. Possibly, Jeanne thought, Down's syndrome made you especially apt to arrange shampoos in the way that being severely depressed made you especially apt to fold towels into geometrically perfect rectangles. Kenneth smiled up at Jeanne as he continued to line up shampoo bottles in precise rows on the shelf in front of him.

"Hi. I don't think we've met," Jeanne said.

"Hi." Kenneth smiled again and then pointed to his nametag, "I'm Kenneth."

Jeanne smiled back and pointed to the area where her nametag was supposed to be. "I don't have my nametag on but I'm Jeanne."

Kenneth and Jeanne had learned of each other's existence. As when two strangers meet, their smiles were polite and their tone of voice mimicked an abstract idea of who they wanted to present themselves to be. And as when two strangers meet, Jeanne had never seen Kenneth again after that encounter. Most interactions with people follow a similar social script: An initial meeting, with not enough time to be able to discern whether or not it was nice to have met, reciting the syllables that have been arbitrarily assigned to their identity and the two parties continue on existing until otherwise instructed.

Jeanne wondered about Kenneth's age. He was smallish, with round wire rimmed glasses. His hair was gray but his smile and facial composition appeared childlike. Jeanne wanted him to change her life.

She wanted him to teach her to be good and kind. She imagined herself sitting next to him on the tiled floor as they patiently stacked shampoos together. She would learn about his mother. His mother would learn about her. She would be invited over for dinner where she would laugh and be good and kind. But, as she imagined this sequence of events, Jeanne was already waving goodbye to Kenneth, starting to walk away.

"Hey, wait," Kenneth said to the back of Jeanne's head. Jeanne turned toward him.

"Hmm, wait, don't tell me," Kenneth said, pretending to think really hard. "Jeanne. Your name is Jeanne." Kenneth started to laugh and Jeanne smiled. Jeanne went on her 15-minute break and Kenneth continued to exist somewhere else.

In the break room Jeanne strategically chose the most isolated table in the far corner. She sat at the table alone, eating a Clif Bar until Anita walked in. Anita was small in both stature and weight but she was very loud. Jeanne tried to avoid interacting with Anita but she was friendly when it was required of her. Out of all the empty tables in the break room, Anita sat directly next to Jeanne. Anita made a big deal of settling herself into her chair and looked around the room wildly. Her big eyes looked like they were trying to launch themselves out of her small body.

Anita's eyes tracked the room and Jeanne's followed. In the corner opposite of Jeanne and Anita sat Zack and Dante. Besides that and the ambient noise of the vending machines, the breakroom was otherwise vacant. The four of them sat, two to a corner, like a school of wayward twenty-something-year-old orphans, wearing matching uniforms and weary facial expressions.

Dante and Zack were in the middle of a conversation about "Dante's girl" who, to Dante's surprise, was pregnant. Before Anita had walked in Jeanne had been listening to Dante repeatedly say, "I need to get a better fucking job, man." At this Zack would nod sympathetically and launch into a speech about how he was joining the Reserve.

At the first hint of a silence, Anita gestured at Zack on the opposite end of the room and said, "Where were you during 9/11?"

Zack paused and everyone in the breakroom watched his facial expression change as he realized that the question was directed toward him. "I was in the 5th grade," he said through a mouthful of chips.

"Oh so you were in school," Anita said. "Where were you during 911?" Anita said to Jeanne with her eyes hanging dangerously outside of her head.

"I wasn't in school because I was asleep. I lived in Hawaii. The time difference..." Jeanne spoke in a deliberate mumble while trying to maintain eye contact with her Clif bar.

"I was on my way to the airport," Anita announced proudly. In the same breath, Anita asked, "Where we're you during the earthquake?"

"I was in my room," Jeanne said. She remembered the earthquake. It was so small that she mistook it for construction work. In the days following the earthquake the first question anyone asked anyone was, "Did you feel the earthquake?" with their eyes big and dangerous like Anita's.

"Where were you Zack?"

"When?"

"During the earthquake."

"Which earthquake?"

"*The* earthquake."

"I don't know."

"Well, I was in the mall. I was in forever 21," Anita said confidently.

"Okay, I have a question," Zack said. "What is your biggest fear, if you had to pick a fear?"

"Launched into the sun," Dante interjected loudly and immediately.

"Why would you be afraid of that? That's impossible," Jeanne said.

"Exactly. That's why I would pick that fear. Because it would never happen."

"No, I meant like, what do you actually fear," Zack said. "Like, out of all the things you fear what would you say that you fear the most?"

"Oh, well, in that case," Dante said, "I don't know. Money. Not being ready to have a kid. Working here for the rest of my life."

"Balloons," Anita answered. "When I was in girl scouts, I was probably 6 or 7 years old, we had a party for being the troupe in our area that sold the most cookies. At the party there were balloons everywhere and I grabbed one. Just as my hands touched the balloon it popped right in front of my face."

Zack laughed. "Can you believe that she's afraid of balloons?" he said, turning toward Jeanne.

"Yeah, she just said it, why wouldn't I believe that?"

"Okay, what do *you* fear the most?"

"Feeling alone and alienated for my entire life."

After work Jeanne drove around to no place in particular while listening to the radio. The radio DJ started talking about a person that took a picture of a man who was dying on the side of the road and then tweeted the picture instead of helping him. The radio DJ said, "There are more important things than twitter" but Jeanne felt doubtful.

Jeanne continued driving while the sun stood brightly, obscuring her vision. Jeanne made a motion to pull down the sun-visor but she had broken it off of her car months ago. Feeling defeated and lonely Jeanne stopped driving and pulled over on the side of the road. She opened up Twitter on her iPhone and tweeted several tweets in succession. She felt depressed. Jeanne didn't know what to do besides tweet when she felt depressed.

"I most closely resemble a cloud in the shape of a depressed human being"

"I want 'insignificant but noticeable' on my gravestone maybe"

"Everything feels extremely terrible and dramatic and normal"

"I feel like I could describe this feeling inside of me for ~20 - ~300 more tweets depending on some factors"

"I feel like I invent horrible situations and emotions in my head so convincingly that I give up on everything before anything even happens"

"Feeling depressed because 6 people unfollowed me and also because I am alive and I am me"

Jeanne sensed herself becoming more depressed after tweeting. She felt lonely after all of her thoughts had left her and were now staring at her on the Internet. Jeanne sometimes felt fearful of posting her thoughts on twitter. After posting a thought to twitter she sometimes thought, "No, I should have saved that." Jeanne felt unsure as to why she would need to save her thoughts. Maybe she needed to somehow save up all of her thoughts, like carnival tickets, and she would be able to one day trade them in for one big, good thing. She could possibly trade them in for a giant stuffed animal with a disproportionately large head that is not a trademarked character but very similar looking to a trademarked character.

She thought that if she ever wrote a novel it would be made up of every thought that she has ever had. She would title it "One Big Good Thing" even if it were small and bad.

Jeanne continued to drive until she reached a small state park. She parked her car and walked over to a bench parallel to the lake. Jeanne stared out at the lake and thought about carving all of her ex-lovers names onto the large stones that sat in the grass and spending her entire life waiting for them to be eroded by the wind and the rain.

In the park there were also children dropping medium sized rocks with both hands into a stream. They fell heavily into the water and sunk down with the sound of small giggles. The children shouted something to their mothers. Something like, "Look mom we're skipping rocks!" The mothers didn't look but they shouted something back like, "Wow good job honey!" The "wow" was drawn out long and slow, more pronounced than any of the other words in the sentence. The children seemed pleased with this response and continued to laugh and throw stones into the river.

A woman sat on a bench across from Jeanne for an extended period of time, folding leaves in her hands like a nervous tick. The woman looked up from her hands and laughed. She looked back down at her hands and looked sad again.

Jeanne felt the urge to ask the woman why she looked down at the leaves and felt sad. Maybe, Jeanne speculated, she felt sad for the leaves that were in pieces all around her. Maybe the woman felt sad for herself because she was sitting on a bench alone and feeling nervous. Perhaps the woman felt guilty because she was laughing while killing something. Jeanne watched the woman as she looked up at middle space and alternated her expression from smiling to sad.

Jeanne thought about wanting to kiss the woman's face when it looked sad. Jeanne wanted to catch her mouth right in the in-between before she smiled. Jeanne wanted the kiss to be sad and slow but hopeful as children laughed and threw rocks with her ex-lovers names into the river.

Jeanne sat on the bench in the park and did nothing. She could feel her heart beating inside of her left shoulder blade. Jeanne wanted to throw rocks into the river like a child and kiss. Jeanne thought, "Kiss kiss," but she continued to sit. She didn't throw rocks. She didn't kiss anyone.

A THING TO DO IS SIT AROUND
AND THINK ABOUT THINGS

I perceive myself to be 15% furniture at this point.
One day I will turn into a nightstand
or something non-essential like that.

I just sat in this spot,
I picked a good spot for sitting on the floor,
watching The Learning Channel
and this show was on—
it was about an obese man who used a Wetvac
to perform liposuction on himself.

I spent the day thinking about gentle foods,
like honey dew.

I WILL WRITE A NATURE POEM ABOUT FEELING GRATEFUL FOR MY MOUTH

I will write a nature poem
about eating corn on the cob and half an oxy
and feeling grateful for my mouth
next to a river
next to a heron
next to a parking lot

It will be about the stagnant canal filled with maggots
There are no fish
Only maggots
They are still alive like we are alive
Wriggling on top of each other
like tiny desperate humans
pushing out the empty space
to feel close to something.
These maggots are becoming something else
on their way to death

And it will be about the lone heron on a rock watching over the
other rocks
It will be about fishing with a 20-foot length of string
and the catch and release of an empty line

This is the laughter:
I am not in control of anything

It might be important to feel close to this
To be able to imagine the construct of a building
without being able to look at one for reference
It might be important to stand next to a river
and then drive home to write a poem about it on your MacBook

It might be important to feel drawn to escape
but pulled back into comfort.
At the first mosquito bite I'm thinking,
FUCK NATURE

I am standing next to a Korean couple.
They are watching the same thing that I am watching
(The River

The Lone Heron
The Maggots
An Immigrant Family Fishing With A Length of String)
but perceiving it differently
and in a different language

i will let you use me
& i will use myself
until i don't remember
whose idea this was

let's ruin shit

IF INSTEAD OF ASKING ME TO INSTALL UPDATES AND RESTART MY COMPUTER I WAS ASKED IF I WANTED TO DIE INSTANTANEOUSLY I WOULD PROBABLY CLICK YES INSTEAD OF NOT NOW

When I am sad, I masturbate.

It feels pathetic for about 10 minutes and OK for about 30 seconds.

Not because of the sensations
but because my hand is in my pants and I am pretending
it's your hand (even though you are right-handed and I use my left)
and you see, still confusing your hand for mine is an embarrassing
thing to do,
even in the dark

Then there is the guilt of wanting you
but only reaching an orgasm when I watch the tiny, naked people
on my laptop

Then there is just the volume. The awful volume of forced guttural
noises
and happiness even on the lowest volume setting

But I need the noises to make it feel real, or perhaps, transparently
fake

I feel like I'm developing (if not already developed) a crippling porn
addiction.

No, no it all feels good, I now remember (having done it just before
editing this poem)

I enjoy the whole orchestra of it: The guilt of missing you
with the nice feeling between my legs with the orb of light and high-
pitched noises emanating from my laptop

This is how I have sex now. I feel very advanced. In the future,
machines will replace humans that I've loved and most other things.
I have preemptively prepared to live without you–for when you can
no longer accidentally return to my bed.

In the two years that you've been gone I have become an extremely advanced human/MacBook/xvideos.com hybrid. This will prove to be an advantage, in the future.

GOOGLE SEARCH HISTORY: WEBMD FIBROMYALGIA, WEBMD LUMPS IN THROAT, WEBMD THROAT CANCER, HOW DO YOU KNOW IF YOU HAVE THROAT CANCER, LIKE, FOR REAL?

It was 7:40 am when I sat down to write this poem.
The time is now 7:41 and I have two lines written
regarding the belligerent nature of time. Four
lines in and I still have not given consent to all this
forward motion. Everything can kill me.
The abstract concept of time can kill me.
Cancer will definitely kill me.
I have a non-specific fear of cancer.
I think, for the average person,
the odds are in favor of not getting cancer.
I am an average person. I will be
okay. And if it is true that laptops somehow increase your chances
of getting cancer, I don't care.
I will just increase my non-specific fear of cancer appropriately.
I am convinced that I suffer
from a mild form of what I have named heart appendicitis,
causing my heart to feel vaguely discomforted for the entire length
of the average lifespan of an American woman.
In old age, when my heart explodes, I will smile
and say, "Finally." Whatever
is going to kill me will kill me
and it will be mine.
I have never died, an image
of teeth biting
into something cold and soft
is something that can make me feel
uncomfortable, but what I lack
in experience I can make up for
in superficiality. And of course,
the downfall of the modern woman
will be loving parents.

the other day i bought some of those perforated valentines day cards, the ones with all the archie characters that you liked from your childhood, and i ripped them apart and used them as confetti

it's your party and i'll cry and i'll ruin it

TRAVEL SOUTH

The window to my bedroom
muffles louder things
that are happening just on the other side.

Though I know that we are just animal machines
that will one day leave
a final task uncompleted,

I want to gather a crowd of strangers to smash and break objects
with their hands.

Through this experience the strangers will create a shared memory
and when everything is broken they can turn to one another and
say, "Remember when things were whole?"

After I incite the crowd of strangers into smashing and breaking
objects with their hands I want to encourage them to just hug and
feel calm.

I want to feel soft next to a body that feels soft
A body that breathes like I breathe:
In and out

I remember when we used to lay on your bed,
stacked lovers,
and breathe into each other's mouths as practice
for when we would inevitably have to live and survive
underwater together

When I get like this,
bathed in the nostalgia of events obfuscated by time,
I could probably walk around my neighborhood
and remember small things about you for
upwards of 6 hours

Now, I appreciate the emotions
that you have toward me
(Of goodwill and continued interest in how I spend my days)
but I wish it could be love
I want to make it love: A concrete feeling
of laying side by side,

not touching
but knowing that you are there as I am alone,
as we are
being pushed apart
at a rate of 5 miles per hour
by a migrating pod of whales.

Every year, starting in the late summer,
the whales begin to travel south

and every year,
the whales move us further
away from each other.
We are suspended in the sea.

This cannot be helped.
This is simply the result
of evolutionary processes.

It is simple, like this:
My stomach goes up and down because I am breathing
and I am experiencing reality because I am breathing

On my own I cannot gather large crowds to form
Nor can I influence their collective actions or emotions
I do not have the charisma
But I can experience reality without breathing
for up to one minute and, for example,
I know this truth:

I can see a picture of an open mouth
and know
that it is Sasha Grey's open mouth

"Mom, why are we here?"
A 20-year-old male rolls a joint in the bathroom of a sleeper train
and smokes it in a New York alleyway.
This isn't the 50's. Jack Kerouac is dead, thank God.
Apart, I open the door to the food court. It swings forward;
It's push not pull.
It's empty but open.

I judge my mental health by how often I water my plant.
I am empty but open. Available,
though the data are skewed. 80% unexplained variation due to
indecisiveness on the part of the researcher.

The radio stations are changing as the 20-year-old male drives
through Cape Cod
with his pretty girlfriend.
"Isn't it beautiful?"
"It's a little gray"
Grey. Gray. The 20-year-old male forgets language with his pretty
girlfriend.
Florescent signs on windows, picture taken from an angle.

"Do you want to take our picture? Let me get a cigarette and look
apathetic."
"Why was she taking a picture of a window?"

The word data is plural, that's the one thing I learned from school.
If I learned other things I won't know until 2 years later
when I'm crying on the steps of The National Mall because I missed
the last train toward Fredericksburg. Street smarts or a centered
compass,
I have neither.

The 20-year-old male is headed back down the East coast.
He is wedged between his pretty girlfriend and a woman
eating Buffalo wings who keeps talking about her swollen feet.
On a train ride from Boston he says my name out loud,
slowly with hesitation.

"The water is fine if you don't mind hypothermia."
A man jumped off a 72 ft. cliff at a quarry,
(Red Granite, WI)
broke the water with his chest and face,
all the buttons on his shirt were gone.

(You're supposed to break the water with your hands
or feet to avoid body impact.)

I could imagine a Godlike figure playing with dominoes
in an abandoned theatre that shows porn on the weekends.

On weekdays the theatre would play an endless loop of black
and white grainy footage of dominoes
toppling each other off of a wooden table then leaping back up
onto the table in the same pattern.

The theatre would be on a street that someone would refer to as
"skid row."
Maybe.

There are some nights
when my heart feels like it is entangled in my throat.
My bones are too narrow.

At 11:47 am, officers responded to East Gobbi Street
and the railroad tracks to investigate a report of an assault.
While there they spoke with Bruce Lee McKinzie, 21, who report-
edly had "nunchaku," or "nunchucks," in his possession.

Don't take the railroad; take the bridge on bike.
According to the Wikipedia article for "Golden Gate Bridge"
more people have committed suicide by jumping off
of the Golden Gate Bridge than any other site.

Bridges are high because ships have to pass underneath them.
The body is falling very fast end over end, spinning
or just floating down at a high rate of speed.

My lower eyelids appear to be stuck to my upper eyelids
via eye crust and separation anxiety.

It seems like every part of my body misses someone.
End over end, spinning.
You can't swim
when your arms are broken.

"He cheated on me." April made her eyes wide and exaggerated to preclude interest in Maria's story. Maria was always telling stories, sharing fragments of her life with April, as if they were friends and not coworkers. Maria and April sat close together on a bench, watching the children play on the playground behind the rec center. Really, they should have been standing but the heat and the kids had beaten them down. Their supervisor wasn't around to supervise either Maria or April, or the kids, so they simply sat and melted.

Maria lived in Hampton, across the Potomac River, about an hour out from their job in Virginia Beach. Once, on a field trip to the Air and Space Museum in Hampton, April pointed to the Potomac River and tried to convince the kids that Maria lived inside of the river with the Loch Ness Monster's American uncle. Maria and April laughed and shared a look between them, like friends. "Alright kids, hold on. We're about to fly," April said, as the bus drove across the incline of the bridge. The bus descended over the other side, picking up speed, and Maria, April, and the 25 5-8 year olds in the city's summer camp program, held out their arms as their voices blended into a chorus of "weeeeeeeeeeeeee." They sounded like strangled, joyous birds. "We're flying! We did it!" April said.

April had to constantly try to turn work into a game where the only way to win was if all 25 kids were laughing in unison. "Look!" April pointed to an old bell tower. They were approaching historic Hampton. "That's where Quasimodo lives." One of the kids asked April what a Quasimodo was. "A Quasimodo," April said, "is a very sad man that lives alone in that tower." April pointed again, for emphasis. "His job is to ring the bell so that everyone remembers that time moves forward. Quasimodo, himself, cannot forget about time. Not ever." The kids looked confused but impressed by her knowledge of Quasimodos. "Shall we visit him instead of going to the museum? He is very sad and lonely." "NOOOOOYESYESYNOOYES," the bus of kids responded.

It was July and the sun seemed to swell, fat and overfull above the playground, directly into April's eyes causing them to produce involuntary moisture. April's entire body was involuntarily moisturizing itself. The wetness sat in-between her shoulder blades and peeked through her blue shirt. The words "The City of Virginia Beach -- Experience the Fun" were highlighted in sweat. "Oh honey, it's okay.

88

You don't have to cry, I'm not sad. I'm over it. He was a bastard. I'm glad he cheated on me," April's coworker Maria tried to console her. Maria's hand made light vertical motions across April's dampened back, mainly hovering but sometimes accidentally touching. She wasn't sure how one could feel glad about being cheated on. It must just be a thing that people say, she thought. She didn't know. She had never been cheated on. April felt like the heat was preventing both of them from experiencing emotions correctly.

"Oh, I wasn't crying," April said as she swiped at her eyes quickly. "It's just that the sun... It's hurting my eyes... One of these kids probably needs a bathroom break by now, right? I'm going to make one of them go to the bathroom. I need to go inside. Fuck. I'm sorry. I'm an asshole. You were just cheated on and I'm complaining about my shitty eyes. Shit. I'm sorry. That sucks. I *am* crying. Really, I am. Shit. This should probably be the opposite, right? Do you want me to rub your back? I just talked a lot at once. I'm sorry. Shit." Maria laughed and continued to touch the air behind April's back. April wiped her eyes with the backs of her hands and grinned.

Maria suddenly removed her hand from the air behind April's back and started flailing it in front of her face. "Ryan!" Maria yelled across the park. One of the boys, Ryan, was revving up to take a running start at the slide. "Ryan, don't you even *think* about running up that slide." Ryan's face looked like the face of a raccoon that was caught in the beam of a flashlight as it was digging through the trash. Alert, but uncaring. "*Ryan*, are you *listening*?" Maria made the word 'listening' have five harsh syllables. "*Ryan*, look at Tyquan. Do you want to look like Tyquan?" Maria pointed to Tyquan and Ryan looked where Maria's finger was pointing. Tyquan had attempted to take on the slide during a game of tag. His squat legs scrambled up the slide as he groped for something to hold onto. Tyquan's hands grasped air as he fell back down the slide, head-butting it with various parts of his face. Tyquan's lips were now swollen and puffed to where his face was 40% lips. His lips hung open like broken, blood-crusted gates. Tyquan noticed Maria pointing at him, waved, and said, "Hi Miss Maria!" enthusiastically. Maria and April tried not to cringe as they watched Tyquan's mouth form words but Ryan was not as tactful. He contorted his face into crazy, exaggerated shapes with his hands and pulled at his own lips to make sure they felt right. Ryan made eye contact with Maria, considered the slide, and then walked over to the swing set.

Inside, the kids formed a line for the water fountain and devoured the metallic tasting water. The water was metallic tasting, to a kid, for a number of reasons. The distinctly metal taste of public water is from various chemical treatments or a lack thereof but each of the kids, uniformly, had a very concrete and recent reference point for the taste of metal. One after the other, they would step up to the water fountain, either bending down, or reaching up on their tip-toes, turn the fountain knob with their tiny hands, and wrap the expanse of their mouths around the spout. The thin skin around their mouths would stretch to accommodate the spout and then bloat as it rapidly filled with water. They would become the water fountain in their eager search to fill themselves of everything. What is this, Miss April? Okay, but what is that, Miss April? Where does the water come from? When I flush the toilet does the water go into here? What if I drink a fish!? Each kid would hover over the water fountain wearily, questioning all of existence, before devouring it.

Toward the back of the fountain line, the kids were getting restless. They started to secretly punch and kick each other with theatrical slowness of movement. There was a group of boys, Conner, Madden, and Billy, who especially liked to punch and kick and dare the other kids to kiss each other. Insofar, they had not succeeded in fostering any kisses but they would not give up, no matter how many times they were scolded. Conner, Madden, and Billy would form a circle around their targets, punching and kicking the air and whatever else was around them while shouting "Kiss! Kiss! Kiss!" They called this Kung Fu. All provocation was simply Kung Fu to a seven-year-old boy.

Conner, Madden, and Billy were the jokesters, the good-natured pranksters, the class clowns. Everyone laughed at their antics. They couldn't help but laugh. The kids were adorable. April could see Conner, Madden, and Billy's life trajectory. They would grow up; they would be athletic and popular, but also smart. Their humor would turn into wit and their round, smiling faces would turn handsome. She would help them become this, April thought, as long as she kept them behind the line, as long as she kept them from crossing over to bullies. She felt a strange obligation to these kids. On a summer weekday she saw them more than their own parents did. For an entire summer she was a surrogate mother to 25 children and she felt it, her feet swelled and her skin sagged deeper. For $8.65 an hour she was Miss April.

Before interrupting the merry-go-round of shouting and kicking boys, April watched them, in an envious sort of way, tilting her head up to try to steal some of their lightness. Kissing is like Kung Fu, April thought, in the way that one person always gains the upper hand and has the option to deliver an open-palm-punch straight to the other's heart area. The boys jumped and kicked and laughed and said the word kiss without any hesitation. They said the word kiss so carelessly, tossing it up and then playfully punching and kicking it. April thought about kissing and wanted to feel the force of three seven-year-olds consistently punching her heart area for the rest of her life.

"Alright, cut it out boys." April jogged from the front of the water fountain line to the back of the water fountain line to break up the gang of boys. At the site of April the boys froze mid punch and tried to affect a look of innocence. "Miss April we were only playing!" said Billy. "Yeah," Madden cut in, pumping up his fists and grinning, "we were just playing kung fu." April wanted to shout at the boys. Stop making my life difficult, she wanted to say, or rather, stop adding to the difficulty of my life. Life felt like too much for April sometimes. She wanted to scream and cry like a child, only to be comforted by a version of her herself, Miss April, that would try to calm her or make her laugh. April wanted to scream "FUCK EVERYONE" until she became light and floating, like a helium balloon.

April looked at Madden. He was pudgier than Billy or Conner, which made him cuter now but would surely morph into a disadvantage in later years. Madden was picking his nose and then smearing the boogers onto his shirt and then onto the wall. She had to get away from him. April knew that if she kept looking at Madden and his boogers she was going to become dangerous. As she watched Madden make abstract art with his boogers, April empathized with school bombers. She felt very capable of bombing a school or at least making an earnest bomb threat. April felt serious and non-sarcastic about bombing a school. She felt afraid of herself. "C'mon, boys," She heard herself saying. "Let's go inside and have snack time." April's voice was gentle and calm. "I think the snack for today is animal crackers but I can sneak some Scooby Snacks for you guys."

men are good
for nothing

men are good
for $$$$$$$

pessimist/opportunist

OVERSIZED T-SHIRTS

What if I'm actually boring and I only know
how to communicate with people [men]
via a hyper-sexualized version of myself?
I'm posting this inquiry
to the conspiracy theory message boards.

Sitting on your couch in my best underwear,
with my hair up and your old shirt on,
I am a small boy swallowed by his
father's clothing
Proud & Smiling.

LOOK WHAT I'VE DONE, DAD.

Last night, our naked asses touched
and that is what we were:
Two Naked Asses Touching

We weren't supposed to do this
We weren't supposed to get naked
like this and then leave our bodies
to look down on ourselves, aerially,
viewing the shapes that our spines
could make together

Now I sit on your couch and project an image
of the word BORING onto your forehead as
if your thoughts were showing through
your skin.
Our fingers,

fractions away
from holding hands,
remain heavy islands

(There is probably a mathematical equation
for figuring out the amount of time spent
staring at empty hands in the average lifespan

For the amount of time that is spent walking past couples
that are holding hands

and laughing

For the number of times I have wanted to scream out to them,
to those filthy hand-holders:

YOU ARE FUCKED UP

And the number of times that I simply continued to walk,
turning
like an unsteady sniper trying
to carefully discern
which pair of hands
could be loosened to fit
mine between them)

You look straight ahead, unflinching,
as I look at you, projecting
more words onto your forehead. Our spines create
shapes unnamable and our faces look sad
but I think that is just the way our faces are.

INSIDE OF THIS POEM THERE IS A ROCK
AND THEN THERE IS ME

Inside of this poem there is a rock
and then there is me.

Outside of this poem the rock is just a rock.
Outside of this poem I am being shot out of a cannon
in an earnest attempt to move my body
farther away from earth.

Just kidding.

I'm writing this poem alone
in my room.

But in this poem, man,
the rock is so dumb.
It has no conception of feminism.
The rock can't even understand the poem
that I put it in but being an object
is better than being a human.

The rock is better than me.
It is smug.

The rock is so fucking smug in this poem.

In this poem, if the rock is dumb
then I am severely disabled.
I am just a human in this woman body.

I want to be objectified. As an object,
I am passive and unmoving
until you move me.

I can be your bitch for cash
I can be new&softbodiedinnocent
and dirty&used
but only if that is what you want

I want to be an object:
Coveted

Craved
A representation
of a woman and a Maybach
in adjacent rap lyrics

An empty glass that can hold

Now, at this point in the poem
I must admit
that I kidded you, again.
I am writing this poem
in my room but I am not
alone.

Inside of this poem there is a rock
and then there is me
(and all of the me's that I can imagine)
(and all the me's that men can imagine for me)
and then there is you
(and all of the you's that you can imagine)

(and all the you's that I can imagine for you)
and then there are strangers.

Right now, on my webcam,
hundreds strangers
have fallen in love with me
and they tell me this
as I pull at my underwear
and place them into a poem.

Jordan's feet met the edge of the steps to the train station. This was her city day. She would go into DC and try to work at feeling cosmopolitan and interesting as she visited the galleries–maybe today she would go to Curator's Office to see the new video installation piece or perhaps she would visit The Phillips Collection to look at the abstract expressionist works–the act of observing was her main intent. Oh how she imagined being a wonderfully fabulous Gallery Girl but surely, she knew, she wouldn't be more than a tourist. She knew the whole idea of it was hopeless and on the morning of her City Day even the sky was depressed, as if it were only concerned with serving as an analog for her disposition, ignoring the rest of the commuters, whose faces bore the mild shapelessness of one who was sensibly resigned. Regardless of personal narrative, large gray clouds shaped like castles and fetuses pushed down toward their heads as they made their separate ways toward the train station. Jordan shuffled out some greeting in her modestly-heeled shoes as she stared at the steep steps that lead down to the station, wondering how the handicapped ride trains. Next to the steps there was a 5-foot long gutter that belly-flopped into a stream of sharp rocks running parallel to the steep steps: a wheelchair ramp for stuntmen. Trains are not for the faint of heart, Jordan thought. She thought about the cliché "faint of heart." She imagined her heart sighing, long and slow, and then falling over from its normally suspended position inside of her ribcage. She felt like that, like a faint heart, most days. While boarding the train she tried to see if she could spot any wheelchairs.

As the train took off toward DC Jordan watched the green blend to the gray, jerk to a pause then rewind as she sped forward, letting something outside of herself control her movement. She felt relief.

Jordan walked around DC aimlessly–forgetting about her glamorous gallery plans–positioning herself in front of shop windows but never entering, while her own plain, rounded, face stared blankly at the higher-cheekboned women that walked behind her at the faster pace of self-assurance. These were the women that were meant to be going off to the galleries to be fabulous. They could be picked out among the tourists as The Ones Who Belonged. After all, she was still trapped in this girlish self-consciousness, which the Gallery Girls had surely left behind. Oh, isn't easy to build a trope of a person and put yourself in opposition to them?

The act of observing was Jordan's main intent. She watched people biking alongside of the cars on the street and people walking their dogs alongside of the bikes. Against a tree that was planted into the sidewalk, she watched two squirrels hump. She wondered if the squirrels thought that what they were doing was provocative or if they just viewed the whole world as the whole world rather than in terms of "inside" or "outside" and "private" or "public." For all she knew, she has happened upon two great performance artists right there. Here was the art! She thought, The Squirrel Gaze and continued walking to escape it.

GIRAFFE. Giraffe. Giraffe giraffe giraffe, Jordan thought. In the middle of DC, [Jordan was unsure as to whether she was literally, geographically, in the middle of DC but the high volume of foot, bicycle, and pedestrian traffic coupled with the concentration of museums and important seeming buildings suggested that she was located in a somewhat central location.] Jordan saw a giraffe standing inside of a giraffe-sized wire pen adjacent to a new apartment complex. The giraffe was positioned next to a sign that said, "LIVE ON THE WILD SIDE."

A crowd of 15 to 20 people were gathered around the giraffe with facial expressions that seemed to suggest that they where also thinking, "GIRAFFE. Giraffe. Giraffe giraffe giraffe." The crowd that was building around the giraffe consisted of small people and large people. The small people were mainly children and the large people were mainly couples to whom the children belonged. The giraffe stood tall over everyone, even the large people. The average size of a giraffe is approximately 3,500 pounds. The crowd of 15 to 20 people, large and small, did not take up as much room in what appeared to be middle of DC, on earth, in the universe, as this one giraffe. Jordan overheard a large person say to his smaller person, "Oh, this is a video of a giraffe" in a confused tone. The smaller person grabbed the camera out of the larger person's hand, pressed a series of buttons on the camera, and then handed it back to the larger person.

Jordan watched the crowd frantically taking pictures of the giraffe while the giraffe stood behind its giraffe-sized cage. Jordan wanted everyone to become calm and silent. Jordan wanted to shout, "LOOK!" and point to something made-up in the opposite direction of the giraffe so that everyone would look at the made-up thing and not the giraffe. Simultaneously, Jordan wanted to calmly lead the crowd into the stomach of the giraffe. Here was her art. She wasn't a

Gallery Girl, she thought, she was an Artist. She wanted to raise her human hands into the air and say, "follow me" authoritatively, as if this was only an extension of a planned tour of DC. Everyone would follow Jordan into the giraffe because it made sense to do so. They would not enter the giraffe through its mouth. Even though the average giraffe is 3,500 pounds its mouth is still not large enough to fit even a very small, small person. To fit inside the mouth of a giraffe a person would have to be comically small, or an infant. Also, even if a small person were small enough to fit through the mouth of the giraffe they would probably get stuck, at some point, inside of the giraffe's extremely long neck. Instead, Jordan would lead the crowd through a hinged door that was located directly on the stomach of the giraffe that had been previously installed due to the pre-planned nature of the tour. The crowd had paid to see the inside of a giraffe and now, Jordan thought, it was time.

Adam's posture is bad, like my own.
Living a long time under
the earth's gravity has increased
the slope of his back to a mild
waterslide. The angle of
my back matches his & I
pretend it is because we are nervous
creatures and we want to appear small.
Put an illusion on something, like two shapes
whose angles create an image
in the negative space, and watch it become
something else.

Adam walks to work and at night,
when it gets colder
because it is October now,
he asks for a ride home
as everyone is released
into the parking lot.
I will take him home tonight.

The streetlights shine
on the tops of our heads.
He walks ahead of me
but he doesn't know
where my car is parked
so he circles back behind me
& I watch the ground
& then I watch his feet
& then I watch his shadow
stretch out
to become enormous.

leave me alone (don't ignore me don't ignore me don't ignore me don't ignore me don't ignore me don't ignore me don't ignore me) come back

i know exactly what i want

CONGRATULATIONS, YOU OWN A LARGE ROUNDED STONE AT THE BOTTOM OF THE SEA

"In future textbooks it will be written
that as a practical joke Pluto was deemed a planet for 76 years
by the experts on all that space matter,"
is my last thought before I turn off my bedside light.

"This American Life" is broadcasting from my opened Macbook.

Ira Glass says, "Money is a fiction" and other words
but I close my eyes and let myself feel
like I am suspended in space
moments before a black hole rips my entire body away from itself.
Panic.

I open my eyes and the hyper-darkness becomes regular darkness.

A calmer sense pushes the panic to the side,
jockeying for the majority of my emotions

In the regular darkness I try to re-locate the light switch
by dragging my face and my hands across the wall.

From an outside source an illusion is projected onto my body
to make me believe that it is never whole.
Accordingly, I extend my arms and fingers to grab at things
and then pull them inward—consuming what I deserve, which is
everything
that I want. It is okay to be selfish because
I can love my perception of self in the regular darkness.

Success.
Calm.

I turn on the light. It's too early to be in the dark.
It is only 5pm.

Ira Glass talks about the people of an island called Yap in the South
Pacific.

On the island of Yap they used large stone disks for currency.

These limestone disks weighed up to thousands of pounds
and as long as they existed, somewhere,
they could still be owned and the ownership could be exchanged
for goods and services

Congratulations,
you own a large rounded stone at the bottom of the sea.

Closing my eyes in the light, making my world orange,
while somewhere else
the experts on all that space matter debate
the two possibilities that exist:

Either we are alone in the universe
or we are not.

Viewed from space I am indistinguishable
from green and blue
amorphous masses.

I can disguise myself with distance
and the concept of perspective.

Viewed from space, one cannot be certain
whether I am an asshole
or a good person
or the entire Pacific Ocean.
Panic.

 Gabby Bess (B. 1992) is the author of the
poetry chapbook *Airplane Food*. She is
the founder and editor of Illuminati Girl
Gang, a publication that promotes female
perspectives in art and literature. She
lives in Virginia.

CPSIA information can be obtained at www.ICGtesting.com
Printed in the USA
LVOW06s0925180813

348440LV00010B/652/P

9 781937 865177